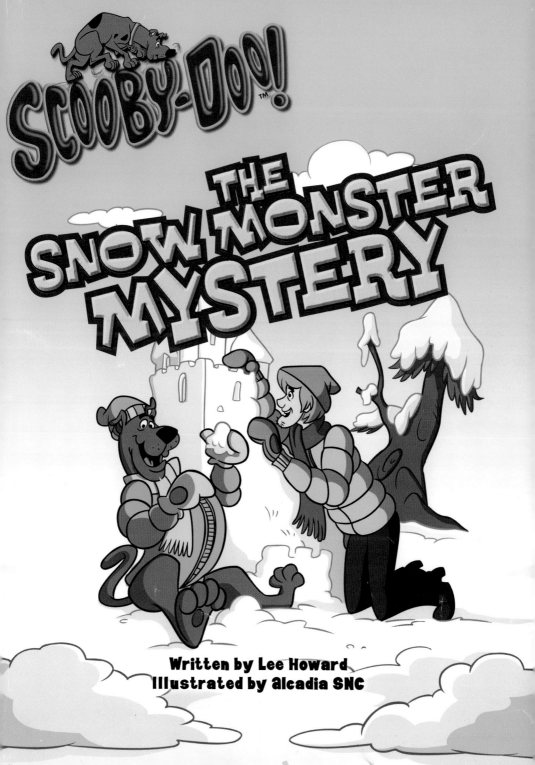

SCOOBY-DOO!™

THE SNOW MONSTER MYSTERY

Written by Lee Howard
Illustrated by Alcadia SNC

ABDO
Spotlight

ABDOPUBLISHING.COM

Reinforced library bound edition published in 2016 by Spotlight, a division of ABDO
PO Box 398166, Minneapolis, Minnesota 55439. Spotlight produces high-quality
reinforced library bound editions for schools and libraries. Published by agreement
with Warner Bros. Entertainment Inc.

Printed in the United States of America, North Mankato, Minnesota.
092015
012016

THIS BOOK CONTAINS
RECYCLED MATERIALS

CATALOGING-IN-PUBLICATION DATA

Howard, Lee.
 Scooby-Doo and the snow monster mystery / Lee Howard.
  p. cm. (Scooby-Doo leveled readers)
Summary: A mysterious monster is putting the freeze on the snow castle contest. Can Scooby
and the gang catch the monster and save the day?
1. Scooby-Doo (Fictitious character)--Juvenile fiction. 2. Dogs--Juvenile fiction. 3. Mystery and
detective stories--Juvenile fiction. 4. Adventure and adventures--Juvenile fiction.
[Fic]--dc23
                    2015156078

978-1-61479-417-2   (Reinforced Library Bound Edition)

Spotlight

A Division of ABDO
abdopublishing.com

"Like, are we there yet?" Shaggy asked, yawning.

"We're here…" Fred said.

The Mystery Machine pulled up in front of a big winter resort.

"Ready for hot chocolate and cookies?" said Shaggy.

"Reah!" said Scooby.

Fred and Velma checked in.

"Rum," Scooby sniffed.

"Like, this place sure smells yummy," said Shaggy.

"You guys can eat after we go skating," Daphne said.

"Isn't this fun!" said Daphne.
Fred, Velma, and Daphne skated.

Scooby and Shaggy fell.
"Rikes!" cried Scooby.
"Like, get me out of here!" said Shaggy.

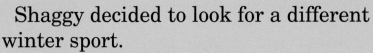

Shaggy decided to look for a different winter sport.

"Like, look at this, Scoob!" he said.

"It's a snow castle contest!" said Daphne.

"I may have to cancel the contest," said Mr. Scott, the lodge owner.

SNOW CASTLE CONTEST

"Mystery, Inc. can help," said Fred.
"Catch the culprit and you get a free vacation!" said Mr. Scott.
"You're on!" cried the gang.

Scooby and Shaggy went to work.
"Jinkies!" said Velma. "What are you building?"
"What else?" said Shaggy. "A fast food restaurant!"

Afterwards, Shaggy and Scooby went to their room.

Fred peeked in. "Bedtime, guys."

"Bedtime?" Shaggy said. "You mean snack time!"

The next morning, the gang went to finish their castle but it was gone. Only a mound of snow was left in its place.

"Zoinks!" Shaggy cried.

"Someone is trying to ruin the contest," said Velma.

"Maybe it was like th-th-the snow monster?" Shaggy asked.

"Hmmm," said Velma. "Funny how only some of the snow castles were ruined."

"It sure seems fishy," Fred agreed.

"Back to our castle, Scoob," said Shaggy.
"We'll make it even bigger this time."
"Rup!" Scooby agreed.

At lunch, Mr. Scott said, "I'm worried. If someone continues to ruin the castles, I'll have to cancel the contest."

"We're on the case," said Fred.

Just then, one of the contestants, named Sam, ran into the dining room.

"The snow monster!" he cried. "He's back!"

"Let's go investigate!" said Fred.

"A tall, hairy creature covered in snow ran out of the woods and stomped on all the castles," Sam explained.

Scooby and Shaggy shook with fear. "Funny," said Velma. "That same snow castle is still standing."

While Shaggy and Scooby were busy rebuilding their castle, the rest of the gang looked for clues.

Near the edge of the woods where the snow monster was seen, Velma found a patch of fur on the ground.

"What's that?" asked Daphne.

Velma picked up the clue.
"Just as I thought," she said. "This is fake."
"I've got a plan to get that monster before he destroys everything again," said Fred.

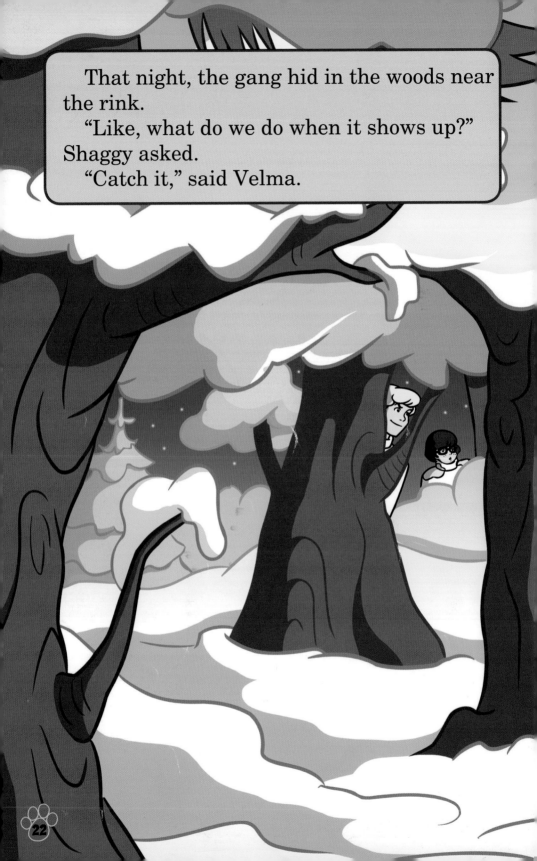

That night, the gang hid in the woods near the rink.

"Like, what do we do when it shows up?" Shaggy asked.

"Catch it," said Velma.

Shaggy and Scooby hid behind a tree.
"I'll look this way," said Shaggy. "You look
that way."
"Rokay!" Scooby said.

A giant wind WHOOSHED around the trees!
Piles of snow fell on Shaggy and Scooby.

Then, the *real* monster appeared!
Shaggy leapt onto a nearby ice tractor.

Scooby pounded the creature with snowballs.

"AHHHHHHH!" cried the monster.

The monster tripped. He slid across the ice rink, ripping his fur.
The gang closed in on him.

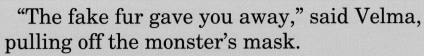

"The fake fur gave you away," said Velma, pulling off the monster's mask.

"Let's see who you really are," said Fred.

"Sam!" the gang shouted.

"I won the contest before," Sam said. "I just wanted to win again!"

"But all the other snow castles were so good."

The next morning, Mr. Scott called Sam into his office.

"You are banned from the lodge," he said.

With the mystery solved, the snow castle contest was back on.

"First prize goes to...Shaggy and Scooby-Doo!"
"Scooby-Dooby-Doo!"